W9-BCM-599

# Treasure
# in the Attic

**Story by Christina Chapman**
**Illustrations by Pat Hoggan**

RSVP
RAINTREE
STECK-VAUGHN
PUBLISHERS
The Steck-Vaughn Company

*Austin, Texas*

I would like to dedicate this book to my parents, my sister Erinn,
and all my family members, who love and encourage me.
Also to all the kids who think they can't do anything; just keep on
trying, because you can! — **C.C.**

To my little family: Nick, Emily, Corby, and my husband, Mike; to
Mom and Dad; and to Diane. These are the people who put up
with my work, help me with my work, and find work for me to do
— the work that I love. — **P.H.**

Printed in Mexico.

1 2 3 4 5 6 7 8 9 0     RRD     97 96 95 94 93 92

Library of Congress Number:   92–35814

**Library of Congress Cataloging-in-Publication Data**

Chapman, Christina, 1980–
   Treasure in the attic / story by Christina Chapman; illustrations by
Pat Hoggan.
   p.    cm. — (Publish-a-book)
   Summary: Having discovered a basket her mother made with her
mother, Sarah wants to learn to make a basket, too, in keeping with
her African heritage.
   1. Children's writings, American.   [1. Afro-Americans —
Fiction.   2. Mothers and daughters — Fiction.   3. Baskets —
Fiction.   4. Children's writings.]   I. Hoggan, Pat, ill.   II. Title.
III. Series.
PZ7.C36637Tr       1993        [Fic] — dc20          92–35814
                                                                           CIP
   ISBN 0–8114–3582–2                                              AC

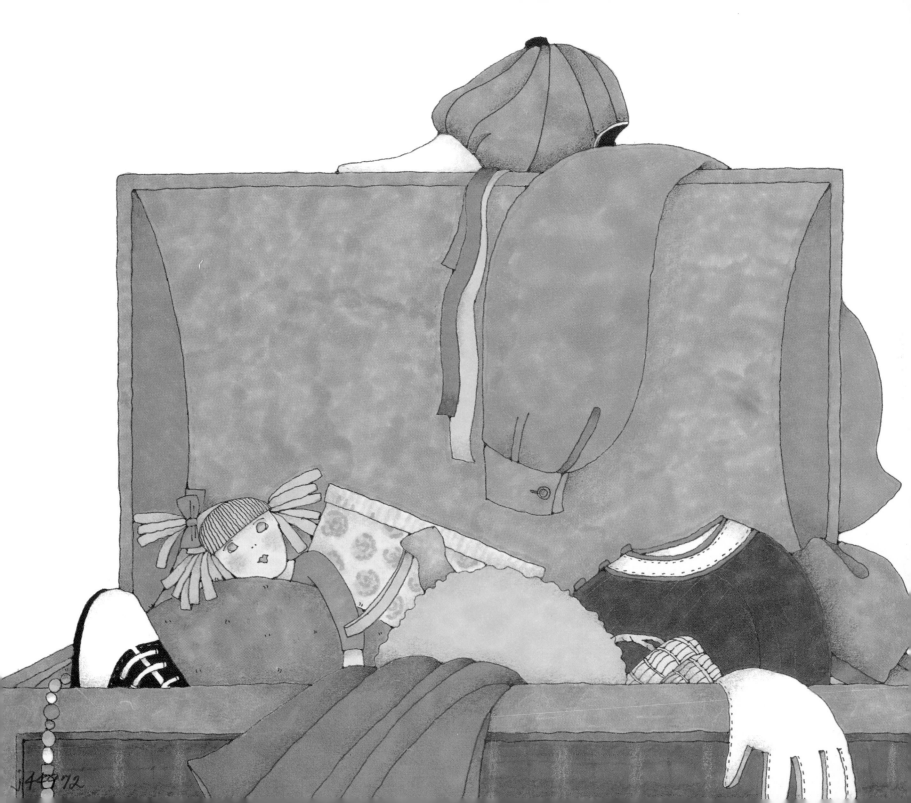

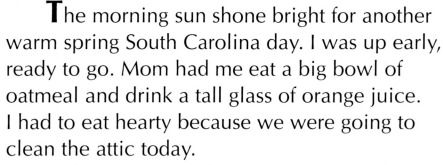

The morning sun shone bright for another warm spring South Carolina day. I was up early, ready to go. Mom had me eat a big bowl of oatmeal and drink a tall glass of orange juice. I had to eat hearty because we were going to clean the attic today.

"Oh, Mom, I just know I'm going to find something interesting up there today!"

"Well, Sarah, you might find something, but I don't know if it will be very interesting," said Mom, looking skeptical.

I excitedly climbed up the steps to the attic with my mother. The first place I headed to was the big, old trunk. I lifted the huge, rusty lid. As I looked inside, I began to laugh at the clothes my mother wore when she was a teenager.

The next thing I found was my mother's school yearbook. I dusted the cover off, trying not to get any dust on me. While I was looking through the pages, I suddenly started laughing.

"Mom, you look so weird in your high school picture."

I went to clear off another spot. Then suddenly I tripped over a book and knocked over a picture. I discovered a cute little basket.

"Mom, can I keep this basket in my room? Please?"

"Oh, I recognize that basket!" exclaimed Mom. "Bring it over here in the light where I can see it. I made this basket with my mother when I was about your age. My mother has quite a collection of these. This one represents a piece of our African heritage."

I was excited and wanted to hear more.

"Well, the art of making this basket was brought with the slaves from Africa to America," said Mom.

I asked her what the baskets were used for.

"I made this one to keep jewelry in. But Grandma has one that belonged to her mother. It was used to store rice. Other baskets were used to store clothes, bread, fruit, and other foods," she explained. "My mother taught me this weaving the same way her mother taught her."

"**C**an you teach me, too?" I asked. "Maybe today?"

"Not today, but next Saturday we can do it. We'll have to go to the country and collect a special grass that we need for the weaving," said Mom.

Luckily Saturday came fast. I put on my jeans and a shirt and got a knife to cut the grass. Mom told me that it would take more than an hour to get to the place in the country. So I grabbed a book to read on the way.

While we were driving to the field, we stopped at a little café for lunch. After we ate our sandwiches, we hopped back into the car. As we drove, we passed fields of wildflowers and cows and horses. Soon we stopped, and we climbed out of the car. I could smell the fresh, crisp spring air. I was glad we were finally there.

I looked over a large, rolling meadow that seemed to go on forever. We walked for about fifteen to twenty minutes until we reached a fairly large square of grass.

"This is perfect. Get out your knife and start cutting," Mom stated.

"What is this grass called?" I asked.

"It's called sweet grass, and it's used because it bends so well and keeps its fresh smell for several years," explained Mom.

19

20

We cut for a while until we had about five baskets filled. My mother went back to the car to get the picnic basket.

"I knew you would be hungry for a snack, so I brought some food," said Mom.

We ate for a while and Mom told me that they did the same thing when she was a child. Mom told me that Grandma planned a day much like today for her, too.

We packed up the grass and headed for Grandma's house to get the special dye and berries to color the baskets. When we got to the farm, Pepper and Spot, Grandma's dogs, greeted us joyfully at the gate. Grandma came walking outside.

"Hello, you two! It's so good to see you! Come inside!" said Grandma.

I asked Grandma if she would show me her collection of baskets. As I walked upstairs with her, I couldn't decide what shape I wanted for a basket. I finally picked round with a lid. After picking out the dyes of red, yellow, and blue, Mom and I drove home. When we got there, it was late and I could hardly wait to go to sleep.

25

The next day, I woke up bright and early. I was ready to make a sweet-grass basket. When I first started, I was really frustrated and wanted to quit, but Mom wouldn't let me. After a few weeks and a lot of patience, I got the basket finished. I was so happy and excited, I wanted to show it to everybody.

27

A couple of days later, a friend of my mother's came over. When she saw the basket, she was astonished. She asked if she could enter the basket in a cultural arts display and contest on Wednesday.

When my mother and I arrived at the contest, I saw pottery from Mexico, prints from Japan, and painted Easter eggs. I saw my basket with a blue ribbon next to it! A few minutes later, a judge asked me if I could teach a class on basket weaving. I was so proud that day. I'll never forget it!

Christina Chapman, author of **Treasure in the Attic**, resides with her family thirty miles north of Detroit, Michigan, in a suburb called Troy. Her father, Robert, is a machine designer, and her mother, Sharon, is a day-care provider. She has a sister, Erinn, two years older than Christina, who is an artist and plays violin. They have one pet, a 17-pound tabby cat named Joey, who can shake hands.

As a sixth grade student at Baker Middle School in Troy, Christina was sponsored in the Publish-a-Book Contest by her teacher, Carol Rexer. Christina was inspired to write this story of a basket-making tradition by an article she read in a magazine. She was quite surprised that she won a writing contest, because writing is not her favorite subject. She really prefers science because she wants to satisfy her curiosity about how things work. She especially likes to do her own experiments!

Christina does enjoy reading and lists among her favorite books the Baby-Sitters Club series, *Guinness Book of World Records*, Garfield books, and Trixie Belden mysteries. Her hobbies include swimming, bike riding, Frisbee, jigsaw puzzles, word searches, needlework kits, painting plaster masks, and computer games. Christina is a multi-talented individual, as she also plays the piano and the cello.

In the future, Christina would like to continue her interest in science and experimenting. Her career goal is to be a science teacher.

The twenty honorable-mention winners in the **1992 Raintree/Steck-Vaughn Publish-a-Book Contest** were Heidi Roberts of Dresden, Maine; Jessica McCulla of Mesa, Arizona; Kristine Laughlin of Mount Laurel, New Jersey; Tori Miner of Franklin, Connecticut; Brittany Kok of Decatur, Illinois; Hilary Manske of Clintonville, Wisconsin; Mandy Baldwin of Bothell, Washington; Kristin Yoshimoto of Honolulu, Hawaii; Arwen Miller of Kent, Ohio; Jessica Martin of Wauwatosa, Wisconsin; Jessa Queyrouze of Mandeville, Louisiana; Kay-Lynn Walters of Fostoria, Ohio; Karen Lauffer of Edgewater, Maryland; Karey Vaughn of Somerset, Pennsylvania; Matthew Kuzio of Mandeville, Louisiana; Leonard Ford of Germantown, Tennessee; Carolyn Hack of Overland Park, Kansas; Emily Levasseur of Hudson, New Hampshire; Christina Miller of Port Jefferson, New York; and Shawna Smith of Hays, Kansas.

Pat Hoggan knew in fourth grade that she wanted to be an artist when she grew up. After attending Brigham Young University to study art, Pat has spent the last eighteen years creating pictures for children's books. She lives near Salt Lake City, Utah, in a home nestled in the shadow of a great mountain range. She thinks the best part of her career as an artist is that it allows her to do the work that she loves and to stay at home with her children.